THE SORCERER'S MAZE
ADVENTURE QUIZ

by

Blair Polly & DM Potter

YouSayWhichWay.com

ISBN-13: 978-1545557228

ISBN-10: 1545557225

THE SORCERER'S MAZE
ADVENTURE QUIZ

How This Book Works

This is an interactive book with YOU as the main character. You have entered the sorcerer's maze and have to find your way out again by answering questions and solving riddles.

You say which way the story goes. Some paths will lead you into trouble, but they all lead to discovery and adventure.

Have fun and follow the links of your choice. For example, **P34** means to turn to page 34. Or at any time, you can go to the List of Choices on **P100** and choose a section from there.

Can you find your way through the maze? The only way to find out is to get reading!

Oh ... and watch out for the shark!

Enter the maze

Your feet are sinking into a marshmallow floor. You take a few quick steps and find you can stay on top if you keep moving. How did you get here? One moment you were reading and now you are in a long hallway. The place smells of candy and the pink walls are soft when you poke them.

There is a sign hanging from the ceiling that says:

YOU ARE AT THE BEGINNING OF THE SORCERER'S MAZE

But how do you get through to the end of the maze? That is the big question.

Down at the end of the hallway is an old red door. Maybe you should start there?

You take a few bouncy steps, your arms held out to help keep your balance. Getting up would be hard. You don't want to fall.

At last you make it to the red door and try the doorknob.

2

It's locked. You pace in a circle to stop from sinking. When you turn back to the door you find another sign. On this sign is a question. Below the question are two possible answers. Maybe answering the question correctly will let you open the door.

The questions reads: What is the largest planet in our solar system?

It's time to make your first decision. You may pick right, you may pick wrong, but still the story will go on. What shall it be?

Jupiter? **P4**

Or

Saturn? **P5**

You need to go back to the previous page and make a choice. That is how to get through the maze.

4

You have chosen Jupiter

Jupiter is correct. Jupiter is the fifth planet from the sun and is 88,730 miles in diameter. It takes 11.9 years to orbit the sun.

The lock clicks and the red door opens. You bounce through.

It's dark in the next room with little lights in the ceiling that look like stars, behind you the red door shuts. Where have you ended up? At least you aren't sinking anymore. Instead you are floating through the air as if there is no gravity. A booming voice begins counting down:

"Ten, nine, eight, seven, six, five, four, three, two, one, blast off!"

Suddenly the room is filled with the roar of rockets. The noise is so loud you have to put your hands over your ears. A streak of light moves across the ceiling, lighting the room and revealing a black door. You push against the wall and float slowly towards it. The new door feels like it's made of metal. Around its edges are rivets. There are some small words stenciled along one edge. The words are another question.

The question reads: Jupiter is the largest planet, but what is the largest mammal on earth?

It is time to make a decision. Which one do you choose?

Blue Whale? **P7**

Or

Elephant? **P8**

You have chosen Saturn

Sorry, that answer is wrong. You can't open the door and go further into the maze. Saturn is only 74,900 miles in diameter, while Jupiter is 88,730.

Did you know that Saturn has rings around it that scientists think are made of ice crystals? Also, did you know that on some dark nights, Saturn is bright enough to see with the naked eye?

Mercury, Venus, Mar, Jupiter and Saturn are all bright enough to see without a telescope, but you have to get away from the city lights. And, if you've got really good eyesight you might just spot Uranus if you know where to look.

If you don't have a telescope, binoculars can help with amateur astronomy too. It's amazing how much more you can see with a little magnification!

But enough facts about Saturn, would you like to try that last question again?

Yes **P2**

Or

No, take me to the correct answer. **P4**

6

Welcome Back to Level 1

There is a sign hanging from the ceiling that says:

**OOPS! YOU ARE AT BACK AT THE BEGINNING OF THE
SORCERER'S MAZE**

Down at the end of the hallway is the same red door.

"Here we go again," you mumble under your breath as you bounce along the squidgy pink floor towards the door.

The door is locked. A sign asks the question you've been asked before.

"At least you should know the answer this time!" a voice booms out, giving you a fright.

The questions reads: What is the largest planet in our solar system?

It is time to make a decision. Which one do you choose?

Jupiter? **P4**

Or

Saturn? **P5**

You have chosen Blue Whale

Well done. Blue Whale is the correct answer. You can open the door.

When you open the door, you just have enough time to take a big breath before you are plunged under the water. As you walk along the seabed, crabs nibble at your toes and starfish crawl across the bottom. Schools of fish swim about, darting from one place to the other like they've all learned the same dance routine.

You try to swim to the surface, but you can't move up. Some strange force is keeping you on the bottom. It must be the sorcerer! But why?

When you look up you see the bottom of a small boat. A rope leads down from the boat to an anchor stuck in the sand not far away. Then you see a shark heading in your direction. And it looks hungry!

You move over to the rope, thinking you can use it to pull yourself up to the surface but there is a note attached to the rope. It says: You must answer this question quickly or you will get eaten. If you answer it correctly you can come to the surface. The question reads: There are approximately 2000 species of starfish, but are they really fish?

It is time to make a quick decision. Which one do you choose?

Yes, starfish are a strange type of fish. **P10**

Or

No, starfish aren't fish at all. **P11**

You have chosen Elephant

I'm sorry elephant, is incorrect. Did you know that there are two different types of elephant? There are Asian elephants and African elephants.

"But what is the difference?" you say.

Well for a start African elephants (like the one in the picture) are much heavier, they have bigger ears, bigger tusks, and their skin is more wrinkled.

African elephants eat mainly leaves, while Asian elephants eat mainly grass.

So how much do you think an African elephant weighs?

It's time to make a choice, but be careful. If you chose wrong you'll end up back at the start. There is a hint in the information above, so which answer do you think is more likely to be correct?

An African elephant weighs 4000 to 7000kg **P9**

Or

An African elephant weights 3000 to 6000kg **P6**

An African elephant weighs 4000 to 7000 kg

What a great answer. You picked the heavier of the two choices. Good skills. This means you'll be able to move on through the maze.

An African elephant weighs 4000 to 7000 kilograms. That's 8,800 to 15,400 pounds. But a blue whale is much bigger. They can weigh 200 tons, (that's 400,000 pounds or a little over 181,000 kg). That's as much as 25 elephants!

It is time to make a decision. Which one of these is bigger?

An elephant? **P8**

Or

A blue whale? **P7**

You have chosen yes, that starfish are a type of fish

Wow, funny looking fish. Where are its fins or gills? Even though they are called starfish (or sea stars), they aren't actually fish at all. They are echinoderms. They got the name starfish because of their shape. Starfish come in all sorts of colors.

Starfish like to eat mussels, clams and other shell fish. Their mouth is on the underside of their body. Some starfish can weigh over 10 pounds!

Now that you know more about starfish, let's go back and try that last question once again.

Go back **P7**

You have chosen NO, starfish aren't fish

You have answered correctly and can pull yourself up the rope. But hurry the shark is right behind you.

When you reach the surface, a boy about your age helps you climb aboard. The boat is small and doesn't have a motor. There are two oars lying in the bottom and a small net with a couple of silver fish caught in its mesh.

"Thanks for helping me," you tell the boy.

The shark is circling the boat but the boy is very relaxed about it so you act casual too.

When you look around, all you can see is water. "How far from land are we?"

"I'm not exactly sure," the boy says. "But I'm sure we could work it out."

"How will we do that?" you ask.

"Well let's see. When I started rowing, I left the beach and went west for 21 miles. Then I turned north and rowed another 6 miles. Then I rowed east for 9 miles. Then south for 4 miles, then east again for 3 miles then south for 2 miles. Then west again for 6 miles.

The boy looks at you and says, "If you answer this correctly I'll row you to shore."

You think hard, trying to work out the answer to the boy's question. "But why are you here?" you ask.

The boy smiles. "Because I'm the sorcerer's apprentice. I'm here to help."

That makes sense. You are in the sorcerer's maze after all.

12

"Hey, it's time to make a decision," the boy says. "Are we 14 or 15 miles from shore?

Which one do you choose?"

Is it 14 miles to shore? **P13**

Or

Is it 15 miles to shore? **P16**

You have decided that it's 14 miles to shore

Unfortunately that is wrong. The correct answer is 15. It's a shame that you didn't get this correct because now you have three more problems to do before you can open the next part of the story.

7 x 8 =

4 x 11 =

5 x 20 =

It is time to make a decision. Which three numbers below are correct?

64, 44 and 90? **P15**

Or

56, 44 and 100? **P14**

You have chosen 56, 44 and 100

That's better. You got it right this time. You can click below
to move on to Level Two.

Go to Level Two **P22**

You have chosen 64, 44 and 90

Oops, that's not right. Maybe you rushed it. You can use a calculator if you want to.

What would you like to do?

Go back and have another go? **P13**

Or

Go back to the beginning of the maze? **P1**

You have decided that it's 15 miles to shore

"That was a tough one. I didn't think you'd get it right," the boy says. "I suppose I'd better get rowing."

He puts the oars into the rowlocks and moves to the bench seat. The shark stops circling and starts bashing the underside of the boat. You hold onto the sides and try to keep it stable.

"Hurry!" you say.

The boy takes the oars and dips them into the water and pulls hard. He is remarkably strong. The little boat glides across the water as fast as a boat with a motor. Soon, the shark is left far behind.

"That was a white pointer by the way," the boy says. "One of the most vicious predators of the sea."

"So that's why you're rowing so fast," you say with a grin.

"A shark could never eat me. I'm the sorcerer's apprentice. I'd just turn him into a tuna and have him for lunch." He points to the fish in the bottom of the boat, "… like those ones."

An hour later, through the mist and haze, you see land in the distance.

"How do you know which way to go?" you ask the boy.

He reaches into his pocket and pulls out a compass. "This tells me all I need to know. But if you can tell me how many degrees there are on my compass dial you can go straight to level 2 of the maze."

But what is the answer to his question? How many degrees are there on a compass? Isn't it the same number as the degrees in a circle?

It is time for you to choose.

Are there 260 degrees on a compass? **P18**

Or

Are there 360 degrees on a compass? **P22**

You have chosen that there are 260 degrees on a compass

"Just as well I'm doing the navigation," the boy says. "There are 360 degrees on my compass, see?"

You squint at the tiny numbers on the dial.

"The four main directions on a compass are north, east, south, and west. Each quadrant has 90 degrees. And, as we all know 4 x 90 is 360."

"How did you work that out so fast?" you ask the boy.

The boy smiles. "Easy, I multiplied 4 x 9 and then added the 0 back on again. 4 x 9 = 36. Add the zero back on and you get 360."

"Wow that's a cool trick," you say. "Does it work with other numbers?"

"Let's try it," the boy says. "You do 6 x 40."

"Okay," you say. "6 times 4 is 24, add the zero and I get 240."

"Correct!" the boy says. "There's all sort of tricks to learn when it comes to making math easy."

The boy stops rowing. "My arms are getting tired. I'll give

you one more chance, and if you get it right you can go straight to LEVEL 2 of the maze."

"Sounds good to me," you say.

He scratches his head. "Okay, try this one. What is 9 x 30?"

You're keen to go straight to LEVEL 2 so you use the trick you've just learned.

Is it:

270? **P22**

Or

180? **P20**

You have chosen 180

"Oops, you got that one wrong," the boy says. "Remember how the trick goes?"

"Umm … I must have forgotten," you mumble.

"Let's try it again," the boy says. "9 x 3 is 27. Then add the 0 back on to the end and the correct answer is 270."

"Oh yeah, I've got it now," you say.

Over the boys shoulder, you notice a boat-sized speck getting rapidly larger. "Hey there's a freighter steaming right towards us," you tell the boy. "I can see containers stacked on board."

"Freighter? I don't see a freighter."

"Turn around!" you yell. "The boat is getting closer really fast. It's going to run us over if you don't move us out of the way!"

The boy just grins. "Well you'd better answer this question correctly then. Otherwise we'll sink and you'll have to go all the way back to the beginning of the maze."

"All the way back?" you ask. "That's unfair."

"Who said anything about the sorcerer is fair? He's full of tricks to trip you up. So think hard and choose wisely."

Meanwhile, the freighter has gone from the size of a house to the size of a … freighter!

"Hurry up," you say. "It's nearly here."

The boy reaches into his bag and pulls out a rock and an apple.

"Right," he says. "Which weighs more, a pound of apples

or a pound of rocks?"

Quick! It's time to make a decision.

Which one of these three answers is correct?

A pound of apples weighs more. **P6**

Or

A pound of rocks weighs more. **P1**

Or

They both weigh the same. **P22**

Welcome to Level Two

A seething mass of ants on the forest floor in front of you have formed themselves into a message. It says: Welcome to Level 2.

You walk around the ants and along a path. Up ahead is a fork in the trail. Standing in the middle of the fork is the sorcerer's apprentice.

"How did I get here?" you ask.

The boy gives you a cheeky smile. "It's the sorcerer. He'll dump you anywhere to keep you from finding a way out of his maze."

"You mean I'll never get out?"

"Oh, you'll get out eventually," the boy says. "It just depends on how good you are at answering questions and solving riddles."

"And if I'm not very good?" you ask.

The boy pulls an energy bar out of his pocket and holds it out towards you. "Here, you might need this for later."

You slip it into your pocket thinking it was good you had

a big breakfast. "What now?"

The boy reaches into his other pocket and pulls out a piece of paper. "This is a question the sorcerer gave me earlier. Good luck."

You suspect you may need it.

The boy holds the note up so he can read it in the dim light coming through the tree branches. "Okay, here goes. Mount Everest is the world's highest mountain, on the border of Nepal and Tibet. What year was it climbed for the very first time?"

It is time to make a choice. Which is correct?

Mt. Everest was first climbed by Edmund Hillary and Tenzing Norgay in 1993. **P24**

Or

Mt. Everest was first climbed by Edmund Hillary and Tenzing Norgay in 1953. **P26**

You've chosen that Mt. Everest was first climbed in 1993

"You were only 40 years out," the sorcerer's apprentice says. "The correct answer is 1953."

"40 years is way out!" you say. "But how was I meant to know that?"

The boy shrugs. "I don't know. Take it up with the sorcerer next time you see him."

"What can you tell me then? Can you tell me how to get out of this forest?" you ask.

"Maybe you can hitch a ride on a bear."

"A bear?" You look around nervously.

"What about a wolf?" the boy teases. "Or maybe an eagle could give you a lift?"

Has the boy gone mad? Why is he talking of wild animals? You half expect these wild animals to appear at any moment. "The sorcerer wouldn't put me in danger would he?" you ask.

"You never know with the sorcerer," the boy says. "Okay it's time for your next question."

You don't want to get this next one wrong so you listen carefully.

"Okay," the boy says. "On which continent would you find bears, wolves and eagles?"

North America? **P37**

Or

Africa? **P35**

Welcome back to Level Two

A seething mass of ants on the forest floor in front of you have formed a message. It says:

WELCOME BACK TO LEVEL TWO

You walk around them and along path. Up ahead is a fork in the trail. Standing in the middle of the path is the sorcerer's apprentice.

"How did I end up here again?" you ask.

The boy gives you a cheeky smile. "When you answer wrong, the sorcerer will dump you anywhere to keep you from finding a way out of his maze."

"How long will it take me to get out?"

"It depends on you," the boy says. "At least you should know this next question. After all you've answered it before."

The boy holds the note up so he can read it in the dim light coming through the tree branches. "Okay, here goes … again. Mount Everest is the world's highest mountain on the border of Nepal and Tibet. What year was it climbed for the very first time?"

It is time to make a choice. Which is correct?

Mt. Everest was first climbed by Edmund Hillary and Tenzing Norgay in 1993. **P24**

Or

Mt Everest was first climbed by Edmund Hillary and Tenzing Norgay in 1953. **P26**

You've chosen that Mt. Everest was first climbed in 1953

"Wow what a good answer," the boy says through a scarf wrapped around his face. "1993 wasn't all that long ago so 1953 was far more likely to be right. Did you know that Edmund Hillary was a beekeeper from New Zealand?"

You pull up the hood of your parka up and shake your head.

"And Tenzing Norgay was a Sherpa guide from Nepal. They were part of a British expedition that first conquered the mountain in May of 1953."

"Interesting," you say. "But we're standing on top of a mountain and it's freezing!"

Why has the sorcerer dumped you way up here? It's just as well he's given you some warm clothing otherwise you'd turn into a block of ice.

The sorcerer's apprentice is laughing. "Quite a view from the top of the world, eh?"

"It certainly is," you say, looking out over the Himalayas. "Hey, how are we breathing up here?"

"The air is thin up here, but we can last a couple of minutes. Imagine what it must have been like to stand here for the very first time," the boy says. "It must have been quite an experience."

There are snow-covered mountains in every direction. The wind is blowing and your nose has an icicle hanging from it. "It's quite an experience right now!" you say, stomping your feet to stay warm. "How are we meant to get down?"

The sorcerer's apprentice pulls up his collar and looks towards a nasty-looking bank of clouds heading in your direction. "Well, we could climb down, but that might take some time. Besides it looks like an ice storm is on its way. We don't want to climb through that!"

You look towards the clouds. "If I solve a riddle, will you get me off this mountain?"

The sorcerer's apprentice reaches into his down-filled jacket. "It just so happens I've got one of those handy."

The piece of paper is very small so hopefully the riddle won't be too difficult.

"Okay, here we go," the boy says. "What stays in a corner, while traveling to Nepal?"

You scratch your head. "Umm … that's a sticky one."

The boy looks at you and shivers. "Quick before we freeze. Which of these five answers is correct?"

1. A suitcase **P1**
2. A box **P6**
3. A stamp **P28**
4. An airline pilot **P30**
5. A mountain climber **P6**

You have chosen stamp

"Well done. That is correct. You can move on through the sorcerer's maze," the sorcerer's apprentice says.

A buzz fills the air and you start to spin around, faster and faster.

"Hang on," the boy yells.

When everything settles down again, you find yourself in a room filled with letters and conveyor belts and people sorting bags of mail.

"Did you know that over 19 billion postage stamps were printed in the United States in 2014?" the boy asks.

"No," you say.

"Did you know that the very first stamp was called a Penny Black, and it was issued in the United Kingdom in May 1840?"

"No," you say.

"Nowadays lots of people collect stamps. Some like to save stamps from a particular country. Others choose a theme like transportation or flowers. Some just collect everything from anywhere."

"They must really love stamps," you say. "But what now? Am I getting near the end of the maze?"

"You've still got a bit more maze to get through. Would you like another question?"

"Sure. After that can we go to lunch?"

The boy nods. "Sure. Do you like pizza?"

"Is that my question? Because that's an easy one!" you

say, grinning.

"No that one doesn't count. But how about this. Where did pizza originate?"

It is time to make a decision. Which is correct?

Pizza came from Italy. **P43**

Or

Pizza was invented in the United States. **P39**

Oops. The right answer is stamp

An envelope suddenly appears in the boy's hand.

"That just appeared out of thin air," you say. "What the heck's going on?"

The boy looks as shocked as you are. "I don't know. But speaking of thin air, did you know that the air up this high has 66% less oxygen in it than it does at sea level?"

"Great! So we're going to suffocate *and* freeze?"

"Nah," the boy says. "I've got some questions in my pocket. Why don't you try one of those?"

"Read it quickly, I'm freezing."

The sorcerer's apprentice pulls out another piece of paper. "Okay this should be easy. What nationality were the first people to climb Mt. Everest without bottled oxygen?"

It is time to make a decision. Were they:

Vulcan and Martian? **P31**

Or

Austrian and Italian? **P33**

You have chosen Vulcan and Martian

"Mr Spock, from *Star Trek*, was Vulcan," the sorcerer's apprentice says. "He was the one with the pointy ears. But he's only a fictional character, not a real person."

"Okay," you say.

"And, as far as we know, there's no such thing as men from Mars, apart from in science fiction, so I doubt they'll be climbing the world's highest peak anytime soon."

Then suddenly you feel yourself spinning at great speed. Colors fly around you head like a million butterflies. Everything goes quiet.

Things go dark and you can't see the sorcerer's apprentice. You can't even see your hand in front of your face. Somewhere in the distance water is dripping.

"Where am I?" you say into the darkness, not really sure if you'll get an answer or not.

"You are in my cave!" booms a strange voice.

"Who are you?" you ask, afraid of what the answer might be.

"I am the sorcerer!"

"Why am I in the dark?"

Footsteps walk towards you in the dark. "Because I don't let anyone see me until they get to the end of the maze."

"Why?"

"Because that's how I want it!" the voice booms.

What's all the mystery about? "How do I get to the end of the maze?"

"You can start by answering this next question. If you get the answer right I have a surprise for you. But if you get it wrong you'll have to go all the way back to the very beginning of the maze."

"All the way back?" you say. "That doesn't seem fair."

"Ah but it's a simple question. You should have no problem," the sorcerer says.

You hope he's right. But for some reason, you don't really trust him.

"The question is," the sorcerer says. "How long is a piece of string?"

"What sort of question is that?" you say. "That's silly!"

"Ha ha ha!" the sorcerer laughs. "That is the correct answer."

"Phew!" you say.

"It is time to make a decision," the voice booms. "Which would you like?"

A surprise? **P41**

Or

Pizza? **P43**

You have chosen Italian and Australian

"Correct! But then you probably know that men from Mars are just fiction, so it's pretty unlikely they'd be doing much mountain climbing!"

"True," you say.

"The first two mountaineers to climb Mt. Everest without bottled oxygen were Peter Habeler from Austria, and Reinhold Messner from Italy."

"Those two must have had pretty good lungs," you say.

"That's right. Because the amount of oxygen in the air becomes less the higher you climb, most mountain climbers start using bottled oxygen at 26,000 feet. Mt. Everest is just over 29,000 feet, so climbing Everest without extra oxygen made a difficult climb even harder."

"They must be nuts," you say. "So where's this lunch you promised?"

With a bright flash and a puff of smoke you are taken off the mountain.

You find yourself in a large room full of people. The sorcerer's apprentice is standing beside you. "I smell pizza!" he says.

You can smell it too. It smells delicious. "I'm hungry. Can we get some?"

The sorcerer's apprentice nods. "Sure we can. But only if you answer this next question correctly."

You feel your stomach rumbling and cross your fingers hoping for an easy one.

"Where did pizza come from?" the boy asks.
It is time for you to choose.
What do you say?
Pizza came from Italy. **P43**
Or
Pizza was invented in the United States. **P39**

You have chosen Africa

"Unfortunately Africa isn't right," the boy says. "Africa has an eagle called the fish eagle, and one wolf species that lives in Eritrea and parts of Ethiopia, but it doesn't have bears anymore."

"What happened to the bears?" you ask.

"There was a bear that lived in the Atlas Mountains of Libya and Morocco, but it is now believed to be extinct."

"How do you know this stuff?" you ask the boy. "Is it because you're the sorcerer's apprentice?"

"No it's because I was stuck in the maze for three weeks and learned lots of things."

"Three weeks? I hope it doesn't take me that long to get out."

The boy laughs. "It won't. I was only five when I first arrived. You're older so you should get through much quicker."

"Phew! You had me worried there."

"But you will need to be clever and work hard to get out," the boys says.

"Well let's do it!" you say.

"Right. This part is a bit different," the boy says. "If you get it right, we go to lunch and have pizza."

"Different? How?"

"Imagine you are standing on a big X looking straight ahead."

"Yeah, okay."

"Now concentrate. Turn to your right. Then turn to your right again. Then turn right once more. Now, turn left. And then turn left again. Now turn right, and right again, and right one last time."

"Okay. I think I've got it."

"It is time to answer a question. If you answer correctly you can go have pizza. If not you're in for a big surprise."

It is time to make a decision. Pick one of these two statements.

I am looking in the opposite direction to where I started. **P41**

Or

I am looking in the same direction that I started in. **P43**

You have chosen North America

"Well done," the boy says. "North America is correct."

"I'm glad of that," you say.

"In North America there are three types of bear. Grizzly bears, which are also called brown bears. Then there are black bears. And finally, in parts of Canada and Alaska, polar bears. Did you know that black bears aren't always black?

"Really?"

The boy nods. "They can also be various shades of brown, black or even white. They estimate the black bear population to be somewhere in the region of 900,000."

"Wow, that's a lot of bears," you say.

"There aren't so many polar bears though," he says. "Only 22,000 or so."

"That still seems a lot."

"Yeah, but that covers a big area. They live way up north in the arctic. Which makes me think of a question."

"Another one?"

"If you want to get through the maze, you need to get them right."

"But I'm hungry," you say to the boy.

"Okay, if you get this one right, we can go have pizza."

Your stomach growls like a grizzly bear. "Deal."

"Here's your question. In which country do most of the world's polar bears live?"

You scratch your head.

"Think hard because if you miss this one, the sorcerer told me I have to send you back to the beginning of Level one."

"But that's all the way back to the beginning!"

"I know. Remember though, if you get this one right you

get pizza!"

It is time to make your choice.

Do most of the world's polar bears live in:

Canada **P43**

Or

The United States **P6**

Pizza was invented in the United States

Sorry, but that answer is incorrect.

The term 'pizza' came from Naples, Italy, back in the 16th century.

However, many cultures ate similar foods well before then. In fact archeologists have found evidence of bread making in Sardinia from more than 7,000 years ago, although the flat breads they made back then would have little resemblance to the cheesy slabs served up in pizza restaurants around the globe today.

"Why did you choose the United States?" the boy says. "Now we'll never get any pizza."

"Hey, you're the sorcerer's apprentice," you say. "Surely you have more questions you can ask me?"

The boy digs deep in his pockets and comes up empty. "No questions, I'm afraid."

Your stomach rumbles. "What's that paper sticking out of your top pocket then?" you ask, pointing.

"Oh, that's not a question. That's a riddle. Would you like one of those instead?"

You nod. "Yes please."

He pulls out the paper and reads: "Billy's mother has five children. Susan, Mary, Thomas and Jack are the names of four of them. What is the fifth child's name?"

It is time to make a decision.

Which of these five answers is right?

Answer this correctly and you can go have pizza for

lunch. If not you're in for a surprise.

1. Mary **P41**
2. Jack **P22**
3. Susan **P6**
4. Billy **P43**
5. Thomas **P1**

Surprise!

Well, I bet you didn't think you'd end up in a long pink hallway that smells of candy. Sound familiar?

But don't worry, you haven't been sent back to the beginning of the maze. You're in a candy land with marshmallow walls and bowls of chocolates and caramels just waiting to be eaten.

The sorcerer's apprentice is sitting in a big overstuffed chair at the far end of the hallway with a big box of chocolates in his lap. "So you found my little secret, eh?" the boy says.

You look around in wonder as you walk towards him. Never before have you seen so many sugary sweets in one place. "But what about your teeth? Won't they fall out if you eat all this?"

The boy opens his mouth to reveal black stumps and swollen gums. "What teeth?" he says.

"Ewww!" you say, smelling his bad breath, even though he's still yards away. "That's horrible."

Then you notice the boy has grown claws where his fingers once were. In a flash, his shirt turns into green scales and a forked tongue shoots out of his mouth.

"Come closer," the creature says. "You look tasty!"

"You're not the sorcerer's apprentice! You're a lizard monster!" you say drawing back. "What have you done with my friend?"

The thing burps. "I'm so sick of candy, I ate him for

lunch."

You're in trouble. You turn and run towards a door at the other end of the hallway. On the door is a piece of paper with a picture and a question on it.

To open the door, you'll need to answer the question. What animal is this?

Make a quick decision. Hurry!
Is this big cat:
A tiger? **P45**
Or
A leopard? **P46**

Yippee, you get to have some pizza!

The smell of pizza is everywhere. But maybe you don't like pizza? Maybe you'd like ice cream or fruit instead?

"In the sorcerer's pizza parlor you can have almost anything you want. All you have to do is answer a question or two," the sorcerer's apprentice says, reading your mind.

"Pizza is fine," you say.

You join the sorcerer's apprentice where he is sitting behind a long table with a group of others.

"I'd like to introduce you to my friends," he says. "This is Billy, Jack, Susan, Mary and Thomas."

The kids all have a similar look. "Are you related?"

Jack answers. "How did you guess? Do we look that similar?"

They not only look similar, Susan and Mary are twins.

"Yes you do," you say, taking a seat.

"Before you eat," the sorcerer's apprentice says, "you've just got one more question to answer. But if you get it wrong. You'll have to go all the way back to the beginning of Level 2."

"Aww!" you cry out. "I want pizza."

"But wait!" the sorcerer's apprentice says. "If you get it right, you get to jump all the way to the end of Lever 2. Isn't that good?"

You're so hungry you just want to get it over with. "Okay what's the question?"

"Okay here it is." The boy pulls a picture out of his

pocket and lays it on the table. "What animal is this?"

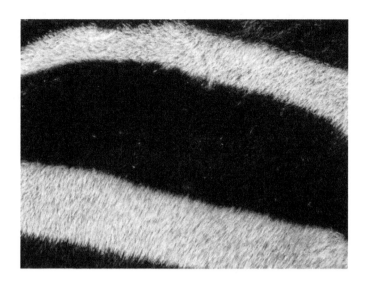

It is time to make a decision.

Which of these three animals is correct?

1. tiger **P25**

2. panda **P41**

3. zebra **P51**

You have chosen tiger

"Aw well, better luck next time. A leopard has spots and a tiger has stripes. At least you'll know the correct answer next time. Let's try another animal question," the sorcerer's apprentice says. "I bet you'll get this one."

"Okay," you say. "But if I get it right, can I go to Level 3?"

The boy nods. "Sure, but with reward comes risk. I'll let you go to the end of Level 3 if you get this right, but if you get it wrong…"

"I have to go back to the beginning?"

"Correct," the sorcerer's apprentice says.

"Okay," you say. "I'll take the chance."

"Really? Without knowing what the question is?" the boy says.

You nod. "I just want to get to the end so I can eat."

"Okay. You asked for it." He pulls a piece of paper out of his pocket and shows it to you.

The question reads: If you mix blue and yellow together what color do you get?

It is time to make a choice. Is it:

Purple? **P25**

Or

Green? **P51**

You have chosen leopard

"Well done!" a voice booms. "That is correct. You can open the door and escape the lizard monster."

You stumble through and hear a reassuring click behind you. There is a thud as the monster hits the now closed door. "Phew that was close!"

"Yes it was!" booms the voice.

You are in a rectangular box. It smells like plywood and sawdust. Light filters down through air holes cut in the top. Wood shavings litter the box's bottom.

The walls are smooth and you can see writing on one of them.

The writing says:

TO GET OUT OF THIS BOX YOU'LL NEED TO ANSWER A TRICK QUESTION.

"Not more questions!" you say in frustration.

In a puff of smoke the sorcerer's apprentice arrives. "I hear the sorcerer had to help you on that last one."

You nod. "Saved me in the nick of time."

"He's good like that. Now don't get fooled on this next question," he says. "Think very, very carefully. This is a really tricky question."

"Is it?" you ask, wondering what you're in for.

The sorcerer's apprentice nods. He looks serious.

"Now think carefully," he says. "How many walls does this box we're in have?"

Walls? Why do they need to know that? you wonder.
It is time to make a choice. Which is correct?
The box has 6 walls. **P48**
Or
The box has 4 walls. **P50**

You have chosen that the box has 6 walls

"Oops. That was a slip up," the sorcerer's apprentice says. "Remember how the air holes were cut into the 'top' of the box and the wood shavings were on the 'bottom'?"

"Yeah but…"

"So the box has a top, a bottom and 4 walls. The tricky part of the question was when I tried to make you think the question was hard, when it was really quite simple."

"That's a bit unfair," you say.

The boy shrugs. "It was a trick. That's what sorcerers do. Don't worry. You've got a chance to reach the end of Level 2 with this next question. But beware, if you get this wrong you'll have to go all the way back to the very beginning of the maze."

The boy pulls a bag out of one pocket. From the other he pulls out 12 marbles. "Right now concentrate."

The boy opens the top of the bag and drops in two marbles. Then he drops in two more. Then he drops in three marbles. Then four more. Then he takes out three, then puts two more back in. Then he takes five marble out of the bag. So how many marbles are left in his hand?

It is time to make your decision. Which is correct?

There are 5 marbles. **P49**

Or

There are 7 marbles. **P51**

Oh no, you've gone all the way back to Level 1

Did you count the marbles in the boys hand or in the bag? It should have been 7 marbles in the boy's hand. Ah well. You'll be a pro at the questions with all the practice you're going to get.

You find yourself back in a long hallway. The place smells of candy and has pink walls that feel like marshmallow when you poke them. The floor is bounces as you walk around. When you don't move you sink.

There's that sign again. It says:

YOU ARE ENTERING THE SORCERER'S MAZE ... AGAIN!

Down at the end of the hallway is a familiar looking red door. You are beginning to hate this door.

You take a few bouncy steps and give it a kick. Then you try the knob. It is locked of course. Beside the door is the same old sign.

The question still reads: What is the largest planet in our solar system?

Which one do you choose this time?

Jupiter? **P4**

Or

Saturn? **P5**

You have chosen that that box has 4 walls

"Well done," the boy says. "Yes the box has 4 walls, a top and a bottom. Were you tempted to pick 6?"

"I was for a moment," you confess.

"The tricky part of the question was that I tried to make you think that the question was tricky when it was really pretty simple."

In a puff of smoke you find yourself sitting in an empty room tied to a chair. The floors are wooden and the walls are white. It looks like an art gallery, but there aren't any pictures on the walls. How did you end up here? It must be that pesky sorcerer again.

There is no sign of the boy. No sounds. No smells. No sharks. No ants.

Twisting your neck as far as it goes, you see a poster on the wall to your left. The printing on the poster is small, but you can just make it out. It is another one of those infernal questions!

The poster reads: You can move on to the end of Level 2 if you get this correct. If you get it wrong you will have to go back to the beginning of this level. Think carefully and pick the correct answer.

The question reads: The blood pumping around your body is called your:

Rotation? **P25**

Or

Circulation? **P51**

Welcome to Level 3

If this is your first time at Level 3, congratulations.

If you've been here before, you'll have to work your way through this level again. But look on the bright side. You're older and wiser this time.

"Well here you are," the sorcerer's apprentice says. "Level three is quite tricky."

"But why are we in the jungle?" you ask looking around at the dense foliage.

The boy acts as if he's just noticed. "That's a very good question."

You expect him to say more, but he doesn't. He just stands there looking at you.

"Well," you say. "Do you know why we're here or not?"

The boy grins. "You're not very observant are you?"

You look around again, trying to spot what the boy is alluding to. But all you see is jungle, with towering trees, ferns, and broad-leafed plants.

"What am I missing?" you ask.

The boy pretends he doesn't hear you and stares above your head.

You look up just in time to see that a huge boa constrictor hanging from a branch above you is about to wrap itself around your neck. You jump back.

"Whoa! Look at the size of that!"

But the boy isn't listening. He is staring off into space his head bent listening to....

"I hear water!" you say. "Should we head towards it?"

The boy speeds off down a narrow path. "Race you there!" he calls over his shoulder.

You take off after him. "Hey, wait up!"

After running for a few minutes, you feel a fine mist against your face. The sound of the water is getting louder. As you come into a clearing you see a towering waterfall.

"Wow," you pant as you look up and up and up. "This is amazing. It just keeps going!"

"It's called Angel Falls. It's the tallest in the world," the sorcerer's apprentice shouts over the roar of water. "Fifteen times taller than Niagara Falls."

You're not surprised it's the highest. The cliff rises vertically for thousands of feet. Little rainbows form in the mist where the sunlight hits it.

"So why are we here?" you ask.

The boy reaches for a piece of paper in his pocket. "It probably has to do with the sorcerer's next question."

Somehow you suspected this was coming.

"Okay, here we go," the boys says. "What country are we in?"

It is time to make a decision if you are to move on through the maze. Is the correct answer:

Brazil? **P53**

Or

Venezuela? **P63**

You have chosen Brazil

Unfortunately, Brazil is not the right answer. Although Brazil borders Venezuela, Angel Falls is well north of the Brazilian border in Venezuela. The falls were given their European name after pilot, Jimmy Angel, who discovered them in 1933 while searching for ore.

Venezuela may have the highest waterfall, but did you know that Brazil is the largest country in South America with a land area of over 5 million square miles? Brazil is the fifth largest country on earth behind Russia, Canada, China and the United States.

"So you chose Brazil, eh?" the sorcerer's apprentice says. "Do you know what that means?"

"No," you answer. "What?"

"It means we have to paddle."

All of a sudden you find yourself in a dugout canoe in the middle of a river. You have a paddle in your hand and the sorcerer's apprentice sits in the narrow boat in front of you.

The river is incredibly wide, the water a murky brown. A huge ship passes, heading upriver half a mile away.

"Where are we?" you ask the boy. "I've never seen a river so wide."

"We're still in Brazil," the boy says. "This is the biggest river in South America. But do you know its name?"

"Maybe," you say. "Are you going to give me a couple choices?"

"Yeah sure," he says. "I'll give you a list of three."

54

It is time for you to make a decision.

What is the name of South America's biggest river?

1. Nile **P60**
2. Congo **P41**
3. Amazon **P55**

You have chosen the Amazon

Well done. The Amazon is correct. The Amazon is the second longest river in the world, only the Nile in Africa is longer. However the Amazon does carry a larger volume of water than the Nile. It runs all the way across Brazil and into Peru.

The boy starts paddling towards shore. "Did you know that the Amazon rainforest has more animal species than anywhere else on earth? More than one third of all the animals live here, and over 3000 species of fish!"

"Doesn't the world's largest snake live here too?" you ask.

"That's right, the anaconda. It's a water snake, so I'd keep paddling if I were you."

You see birds sitting in the trees lining the shore. There are splashes in the river around you. "It's probably got the most insects too!" you say, swatting at a mosquito that's landed on your arm. "Got any bug spray?"

The boy rustles in his pockets and pulls out a tube of insect repellent while the canoe rocks back and forth. "Here, try some of this; the mosquitoes around here carry all sorts of diseases. Yellow fever, malaria, dengue fever, and more. Did you know more people get killed by mosquitoes every year than all the snakes and lions and wolves, alligators and spiders put together?"

"Really?" you say, quick to get the top off the tube and spread the cream on your arms, neck, and face. "So why did the sorcerer put us here?"

"Oh, he has his reasons. When we get to shore I'll tell you."

You pass the repellent back to the boy. Then grabbing your paddle you follow the boy's lead and make long strokes through the water. Ten minutes later you and the boy are pulling the dugout up onto the bank of the river.

"Come this way," the boy says, heading off into the jungle. "I want to show you something."

The jungle is thick. And there are strange noises everywhere. High up in the canopy, a group of monkeys with thin arms and legs and long tails leap about gathering food and going about their lives. They are very agile and move around the treetops with ease.

"Would you like a question?" the sorcerer's apprentice asks. "You do want to finish the maze don't you?"

"Okay," you say but actually this is a pretty cool place and you're enjoying the visit.

The boy nods and pulls a piece of paper out of his pocket. "Which of the following is a type of monkey?"

It is time to make a decision. Which of these five do you choose?

1. bird monkey **P59**
2. alligator monkey **P41**
3. scorpion monkey **P59**
4. spider monkey **P57**
5. lizard monkey **P6**

You have chosen spider monkey

"Well done," the sorcerer's apprentice says. "Those are definitely spider monkeys up there. Now all you have to do is answer one more question and you've made it to Level 4. Isn't that exciting?"

"I did like the jungle though," you say, looking at your new surroundings. "What's with all this sand?"

The sorcerer's apprentice looks around. "Hmmm … this is weird."

"You mean you don't know where we are?"

"Oh I know. We're in the Sahara Desert. It's just that I could have sworn I parked my camel here."

"Your camel?"

"Well you don't want to walk 300 miles in this heat do you?"

You turn and look around. For as far as you can see, all you see is sand. "300 miles? Are you serious?"

"I told you the sorcerer was tricky. He wants you to stay a while longer, so he's making it difficult for you."

"But what did I do to him?"

"That's not the point. You're making it through his maze too quickly and he doesn't like that. He prides himself on making hard mazes and if you get though too easily he just gets trickier."

"Does that mean…?"

"…that the next question will be more difficult? Yes. I suspect this next one will be a real stinker. But remember if you get it right, you'll be at Level 4."

"And if I don't?"

"Then you've got a bit of a walk in front of you. And you'll have to do it on your own, because I've got an appointment elsewhere."

This is not what you want to hear. If you're left in the Sahara all alone you'll probably die of thirst.

"Okay here it is. Choose carefully now," the boy says. "Do the camels of North Africa, where the Sahara Desert is, have one hump or two?"

"How should I know?" you say. "I'm not an expert on camels!"

"Would you like a hint?" the boy asks.

"Yes please," you say.

"The answer is less than three."

"What! That's a very odd hint."

"Exactly!" the boy says with a big grin. "An odd question indeed."

What is he trying to tell you with this cryptic clue? It's all very odd.

"It is time to make a decision," the boy says. "If you get it right, you'll make it to Level 4. But if you get it wrong. It's back to the beginning of Level 3 for you."

So, which is correct?

Camels of the Sahara have one hump. **P74**

Or

Camels of the Sahara have two humps. **P51**

Oops, that is not the name of a monkey

Would you like to:
Try that question again? **P56**
Or
Go to Level 3? **P51**

60

You have chosen the wrong river

Both the Nile and the Congo are rivers in Africa.

The Nile is the longest river in the world, while the Amazon carries the largest volume of water.

You wish you'd known this before because now you've been sucked up by a swirling tornado and carried up into the sky.

You close your eyes to protect them from the dust and hope the sorcerer drops you somewhere safe. As the tornado spins faster and faster, you fly higher and higher.

Then someone grabs your hand.

It's the boy.

"Did you know tornados can pick up whole trucks and cars and throw them about like toys?" the sorcerer's apprentice yells over the howling wind.

"What? I can't hear you!" you yell back.

Then, as quickly as it started, the wind stops and you're

F
A
L
L
I
N
G

The ground is far below and houses look like pieces of Lego.

"Pull the rip cord!" the sorcerer's apprentice yells.

"Quickly, or you'll hit the ground with a splat!"

You look down at your chest and see a sturdy metal handle with a cord attached to it.

"Just yank it hard!" the boy yells.

With a tug, the cord releases your parachute and your freefall jerks to a halt. Above you billows a brightly colored parachute.

The boy, hanging below a chute of his own gives you the thumbs up. "That sorcerer's a bit of a comedian at times," he says. "The first time I went through the maze I nearly pooped myself."

"Yeah, the sorcerer's funny all right. Funny in the head if you ask me."

"Now to avoid breaking your legs you're gonna want to bend your knees and roll when you land," the boy says, pulling on his ropes to steer his chute past a fence and into a big field of grass.

You do the same. The ground is coming up fast.

"Oomph," you grunt as you hit the grass and roll.

The boy detaches his harness and runs over to help you with yours. "Wasn't that fun?" he asks.

"Yeah, right. I love being sucked up into the sky and then dropped from a great height when I'm not expecting it."

The boy shrugs. "You get used to it."

"You mean it might happen again?"

"You never know with the sorcerer. In the meantime," the boy says pulling a piece of paper out of his pocket. "The sorcerer wants me to ask you a question."

You exhale long and slow. You need to concentrate and get this right so you can get through this crazy maze.

"Right," the boy says. "If you get this correct, you get to start Level 4. But you have to go all the way back to the beginning of Level 3 if you get it wrong.

"Okay you say. What's the question?"

"Right. Who were the first people credited with heavier-than-air powered flight?"

It is time to make a decision. Which is right?

The Boeing Brothers were the first to fly. **P51**

Or

The Wright Brothers were the first to fly. **P74**

You have chosen Venezuela

Well done, you got it right. At a height of 3,212 feet, Angel Falls is in the Canaima National Park in Venezuela. First discovered by Europeans in the 1930s by a pilot named Jimmy Angel.

"So, have you been to Venezuela before?" the sorcerer's apprentice asks.

"Why?" you ask. "Have you got more questions to ask me?

The boy laughs. "How did you know?"

"Just a lucky guess. Doh! Tell me, did the sorcerer use to be a travel agent by any chance?"

The boy shakes his head. "Not that I'm aware of. He does send me around the world a bit though. One of the perks of the job I guess."

"You mean you get paid for doing this?" you ask.

"Well of course. There's a minimum wage law and the sorcerer isn't a criminal."

"So how much do you get an hour?" you say, wondering if there are any vacancies.

"Well I could give you the weekly rate and you could work it out. How's that?"

That seems fair. "Yeah, okay."

"And," the boy says. "If you get this right, you can move on through the maze."

"And if I don't?"

"Well … back to the beginning of Level 2 for you!"

You frown at the boy. "Just what I was afraid of."

"Okay here's your question. If I work on a Saturday, I get time and a half. Last Saturday I earned $96 for an eight hour day. What is my normal hourly rate?"

It is time to make a decision. Is the boy's normal hourly rate:

$8.00 per hour **P65**

Or is it:

$12.00 per hour **P115**

(You can use a calculator if required)

You chose $8 per hour

"Well done," the sorcerer's apprentice says. I usually earn 8 dollars an hour but time and a half on a Saturday is $12 per hour and 8 times 12 is 96."

The boy leads you through a thick purple fog. When the fog clears you are standing in the biggest shopping mall you've ever seen and your clothes smell of grape jelly.

"Where did the jungle go?" you ask the sorcerer's apprentice.

"It's back in South America," he replies. "We're in Dubai."

"I've heard of Dubai, but I'm not that sure where that is," you say, looking around at all the shops."

"Well that's okay, because Dubai has nothing to do with the next question. I just came to buy some socks."

"Socks?" you ask.

"The next question is about math. Not socks though," the boy says, popping into a nearby shop.

That is not what you wanted to hear. But at least you figure you'll have a 50/50 chance of getting the next one right.

The boy comes out of the shop holding a small parcel in his hand. "You're probably thinking you've got a 50/50 chance with this next question don't you?" the boy says.

"How do you do that?" you say. "Seems an unfair advantage being able to read my mind."

"It was just an educated guess. Mind reading is just

trickery, it's not real."

You pretend to agree with him, but you're not so sure. "Okay, well let's get it over with. What's the question?"

"This one is more a test in observation. Just pick the number that's different."

He points to the glass window of the nearest shop. On it are lots of numbers. "This should be easy. Which one is different?"

1 **P115**

2 **P67**

3 **P41**

5 **P116**

7 **P70**

9 **P68**

11 **P70**

13 **P67**

You have chosen the wrong number

"If you chose number 2 because it was the only even number, that was a good try," the sorcerer's apprentice says. "But that's not the number I'm looking for. This is a tricky question, you'll have to think harder."

"But is it really tricky, or are you trying to trick me by telling me it's tricky?" you ask.

The boy smiles. "Do you want to try again, or should I just tell you the correct answer?"

Do you:

Try again **P66**

Or

Skip this question and go to the correct answer. **P68**

Or

Take a chance and go to **P115**

You have correctly chosen number 9

Well done. Yes, 9 is different from all the other numbers because it's the only one that isn't a prime number.

What is a prime number?

Well, a prime number is a number than can only be divided by itself and the number 1.

17 is also a prime number. Can you guess which prime number is the one after 17? Remember it won't be an even number because you can divide all even numbers by 1 and 2 so it can't be prime.

But if you picked 19 you were right. So that gives us 1, 2, 3, 5, 7, 11, 13, 17, 19 ... they go on and on, but they get harder and harder to find as they get bigger. How many numbers can you find that can only be divided by 1 and the number itself?

In a puff of black smoke, the sorcerer's apprentice arrives. He coughs and his face is covered in soot.

"Where have you been?" you ask. "You're all dirty."

The boy brushes off his clothes and wipes his face with a tissue. "I've been shoveling coal."

"Why?" you ask. "Was the sorcerer punishing you?"

"No the sorcerer was cold and he's got a coal boiler to heat his cave in the winter."

You look at the boy. "But why doesn't he live in a proper house. Surely it would be much warmer than a damp cave?"

"But he quite likes living in a cave," the boys says. "He was born in a cave and he feels he needs to carry on sorcerer traditions."

"But why?" you ask. "Why would he do that when much warmer houses have been made? Just because something's old doesn't make it better. We learn how to do things better all the time. Take medicine for example."

"Speaking of which, the sorcerer has given me a question to ask you. It's about old stuff too."

"Old stuff?"

"Yes. And this is an important one too. If you get it wrong, the sorcerer said he's going to send you all the way back to the very beginning of the maze."

"What? All the way back to Level 1?

"I'm afraid so. The sorcerer likes having you around. He doesn't have many friends."

"But we haven't even met," you say. "How can he like me?"

The boy smiles. "My reports of course."

"Oh well. I suppose you'd better give me the question," you say. "No point in wasting time if I'm going to have to work my way all the way through the maze again."

"Okay, here goes. What is coal made from?"

"The stuff you've been shoveling?" you ask.

"Yep."

It is time for you to make a decision. Which of the following answers is correct?

Coal comes from ancient trees and plants. **P71**

Or

Coal is a type of rock made inside a volcano. **P70**

You are back at the start

In a puff of pink smoke, you find yourself standing on mushy marshmallow. You and the boy bounce from spot to spot avoid sinking in. The sign hanging on the wall says:

YOU ARE AT THE BEGINNING OF THE SORCERER'S MAZE

Down at the end of the hallway is the same ugly old red door.

"I wish I could get a different colored door for a change," you say.

"Be careful what you wish for in the sorcerer's maze," the boy says. "You might get more than you bargained for."

You bounce over to the door and try the handle. Of course it's locked, just like last time. Is it the same question you were asked before? Yes! Well at least you'll know the answer this time.

The questions reads: What is the largest planet in our solar system?

Which one do you choose?

Jupiter? **P4**

Or

Saturn? **P5**

"Would you like to have that one over again?" the boy says. "I like you. And I am here to help. What do you say?"

Yes I want to have another go at that last question. **P69**

Coal is made from ancient trees and plants

Well done that is correct. Coal was formed long before the dinosaurs when layers of plant material was laid down in swamps. As the layers were buried they were pressed by the weight of the earth into the coal we burn today. Coal is a very dirty way to get energy and creates lots of greenhouse gasses.

"So now you know a bit about coal," the sorcerer's apprentice says. "But did you know that oil is made from plant material too? That's why they are both called fossil fuels."

"Is that why we're in Texas?"

"Very good," the boys says. "How did you know we've been transported to Texas?"

"The 'Welcome to Texas' sign behind you was a big clue," you say smugly.

The boy turns around. "Oh, I didn't see that. So you're not so clever after all."

"Does that mean my next question is about Texas?" you ask.

"You're getting the hang of this game," the boy says. "Did you know that until Alaska joined the union Texas was the largest state?"

"Yeah I heard that," you say.

"But do you know how the United States got Alaska?"

"Is this my next question?"

The boy nods. "Yes, and if you get it correct, you get to

go to the beginning of Level 4. How's that?"

It is time to make a decision. Which of the following is correct?

The U.S. bought Alaska from Russia in 1867. **P74**

Or

Alaska was taken from Japan at the end of World War 2.
P73

Alaska was taken from Japan at the end of World War 2

Unfortunately, this is incorrect. Alaska was purchased from Russia in 1867 but didn't become a state until 1959.

You look around and wonder where you are. It is suddenly very hot and dry. The ground around you is sandy and there are cattle munching on the sparse grass.

"Where are we now?" you ask the sorcerer's apprentice. "Are we back in Texas?"

"Close, but not quite."

"New Mexico?"

The boy shakes his head

"Oklahoma?" you ask.

"Nope."

"Arkansas?" you guess.

"Nope."

"Well we can't be in Mexico because that stop sign over there is in English, not Spanish."

The boy smiles. "There is one more state that borders Texas. If you get this right you get to go to the beginning of Level 4. However if you get it wrong ... well let's not think about that."

It is time to make a decision. Which of these three states borders Texas?

Arizona **P51**

Mississippi **P115**

Or

Louisiana **P74**

Welcome to Level 4

"Wow, you're doing pretty well," the sorcerer's apprentice says. "You've made it to the last level."

"Yes!" you say, pumping your fist in the air.

"But now you've got some quick decisions to make in the final rush to the end."

You look down the long hallway. It is lined with different colored doors. "What are all the doors for?"

"Only two of them work from this side. All the others can only be opened from the other side." The boy points to the end of the hallway. "To start, you can choose either the red door or the green door."

"And what happens if I choose wrong?" you ask.

"Well you'll be in this part of the maze for quite some time. Try to remember your path and you might make it out again."

"Aren't you coming with me?"

The boy shakes his head. "I've got other work to do. From here on it's up to you."

You walk down the hallway past doors of various colors. Finally you come to a red door and a green door. You turn around to wave goodbye to the boy, but when you look back, he's already gone.

You scratch your head. Which door do you choose? Does green mean go and red mean stop? Or is this another one of the sorcerer's tricks?"

It is time to make a decision. Which door do you open?

Open the red door. **P76**

Or

Open the green door. **P77**

You have chosen the red door

You are in near darkness. The walls are slimy. It smells like a sewer. You hear the squeak of rats and feel something scurrying around your feet.

The ground at your feet is hard like concrete. You run from the rats. Finally you turn a corner. In front of you are two doors. One is yellow and one is orange.

More rats have found you. They are getting bolder, coming closer.

Quick, which door do you take?

Take the yellow door. **P78**

Or

Take the orange door. **P79**

You have chosen the green door

Behind the green door is a dark room with a jungle scene painted on its walls. You look around for some more doors, but they are disguised. You hear a deep throated roar, but when you look around you can't see where the noise is coming from.

You reach out and run your hands along the wall. Maybe you'll be able to feel the knob? You start moving around the walls feeling for as you go, but after a few minutes you give up.

Then you spot something interesting. There are two little buttons painted to look like tiny flowers.

One of the buttons says UP, and the other says DOWN.

You take a moment to think. Then you see a tiger sitting quietly in the corner. The tiger is staring at you. It licks its lips and stands up. It moves towards you … stalking you.

Quick, push a button!

Do you:

Push the up button? **P80**

Or

Push the down button? **P81**

You have chosen the yellow door

Beyond the yellow door is a long hallway lined with mirrors. You see your reflection and it seems to go on forever.

After walking down the hallway, you come to a junction. You turn right and keep walking. You seem to be walking in circles but then, finally you see two doors in the distance. A blue door and a purple door.

But which door do you take?

Take the blue door. **P83**

Or

Take the purple door. **P82**

You have chosen the orange door

You are in a round room with blue and white tiles on the floor. What a strange place. On the walls are a series of pipes protruding into the room. On the wall are two doors, one pink and one brown.

What should you do? You are starting to wish there were questions to answer because choosing doors is just luck.

As you think about which door to choose, water starts to pour out of the pipes. This room must be a swimming pool, but there is a roof on it. What happens when the pool fills up? There won't be any air left.

The water is gushing in faster and faster. It is cold and already up to your neck. Quick, before you drown! Choose a door!

Open the pink door. **P83**

Or

Open the brown door. **P86**

80

You have pushed the up button

After pushing the UP button, a sliding door opens. You rush inside and hide from the tiger. Thankfully the door closes again just before the tiger pounces. You hear the tiger's claws scratching on the outside of the door as the lift takes off.

Siberian tigers can weigh up to 675 pounds. You wouldn't last long if one of those got hold of you.

The elevator travels up and up. Finally it stops and the doors open again

"Oh no!" you cry out. "I've gone around in a circle!"

You are back in the hallway of doors.

Looks like it time to start again. So which door do you take this time?

The green door? **P77**

Or

The red door? **P76**

You have pushed the down button

After pushing the down button, a sliding door opens. You jump inside the lift and the doors slam shut just as the tiger leaps towards you.

Down, down, and down you go. Then with a jerk, you come to a stop. But the door doesn't open.

You wait for a while longer, but still the door doesn't open. What are you going to do?

The only button on the inside of the lift is an UP button, but there is a tiger up there. You don't want to go up again surely?

Then you see them. A trap door in the floor of the lift and another tiny door in the back wall that is only as high as your knees.

What do you do? Do you:

Go through the trap door? **P88**

Or

Go through the tiny door? **P83**

You have chosen the purple door

You're standing in a long metal box. It is cold and there is ice on the walls. The floor is a little sloped and you are sliding downhill, not quickly, but because you've got nothing to hold on to, you can't stop.

You hold out your arms to keep your balance as you slide.

Then you see a metal ladder attached to the wall. Above the ladder, there is a trap door in the ceiling. Opposite the ladder is a round porthole with a big metal handle, like those you'd see in a submarine.

It is freezing. Your arms are covered in goose bumps.

You need to choose quickly before you turn into ice. Do you:

Climb the ladder? **P84**

Or

Open the porthole? **P83**

You are back in the hallway of doors

How did that happen? You must have taken a wrong turn somewhere.

You look around but the sorcerer's apprentice is nowhere to be seen.

Looks like you're starting over again.

You walk down the long hallway. Past door after door. Only two of them have doorknobs.

Which door do you take?

The green door? **P77**

Or

The red door? **P76**

You have chosen to climb the ladder

You open the trap door at the top of the ladder and haul yourself up. You find yourself in a long narrow passageway. The walls are covered in spiders. Hundreds of big brown hairy spiders. Some of them skitter towards you. You try to go back, but the trap door has shut and there is no handle on this side. What are you going to do?

Then, down at the end of the hallway you see two doors. You run, brushing spiders off you as you go.

One of the doors is red the other is black. Just like the colors of a black widow spider. But which do you choose?

Quick the spiders are getting closer! Choose a door!

Choose the red door. **P76**

Or

Choose the black door. **P85**

You have chosen the black door

You smell pizza as soon as you enter the next room and slam the black door shut. The room is large with a big window in one wall. On the other side of the window the sorcerer's apprentice is eating pizza with 5 others. Two of them are twins. It feels like you've been here before.

It's been hours since you've had any food.

You knock on the window but nobody can hear you. There are no doors that you can see but at the end of the room is a hole in the wall. Maybe that is the way to get out of this maze.

As you walk towards the hole, you see a trap door in the floor. Maybe the trap door is the better way to go?

It is time to make a decision. Do you:

Go through the hole in the wall? **P93**

Or

Go down through the trap door? **P88**

You have chosen the brown door

You can still hear water running behind you. A few drops seep under the brown door even though it's closed firmly behind you.

It is gloomy in this room. Then you see a light switch on the wall beside you. You turn it on.

Oh no! There are doors everywhere. And if that wasn't bad enough, it smells horrible. Like a hundred people have farted all at the same time!

You try to hold your breath, but you know you need to get out as soon as possible.

But which of the six doors do you choose?

Green **P77**

Red **P76**

Yellow **P78**

Purple **P82**

White **P87**

Blue **P83**

You have chosen the white door

This is the longest hallway you've seen yet. It seems to go on forever. As you walk you see pictures of the boy doing different activities. In one picture he is parachuting, in another he is standing on top of a mountain. In the next, he is standing at the foot of a massive waterfall, and at another, he is playing with a long-armed monkey up in a tree.

Then you notice that you're in some of the pictures too. What is going on here?

After walking for ten minutes, you finally see a couple of doors. One has yellow dots on it. The other has blue stripes. Then music starts to play. It sounds like a circus is in town.

Which door do you choose?

Choose the door with the yellow spots. **P83**

Or

Choose the door with the blue stripes. **P89**

You have decided to go through the trap door

The air is cool down here. The walls are made of stone and there are burning torches every few yards along the passageway so you can see where you are going.

At the end of the passage stands a shiny suit of armor, complete with spear. It looks about your size. You wonder if the sorcerer has put it there for a reason, or if it's just decoration. Beside the armor lays a double-edged axe.

When you see a sign that says BEWARE OF THE DRAGON you start to worry.

Maybe you should put the suit on, but then how? You'd need someone to help you do up the back.

Instead you pick up the axe and creep slowly forward.

At the end of the passageway are two huge doors, one of wood and one covered in beaten copper.

When you hear the hiss of the dragon behind you, you realize you've got to move quickly. Flames lick around your feet. You drop the axe and run towards the doors. But which do you open?

The wooden door? **P115**

Or

The copper door? **P91**

Go through the door with the blue stripes

Now you seem to be getting somewhere.

You find yourself in a luxurious room filled with plush furniture.

There is a big screen TV on one wall and a fridge in the corner. You're over to the fridge in a flash to see what's inside.

You reach into the freezer compartment and grab a popsicle.

As you eat, the TV flickers to life. You see an old white-haired man on the screen dressed in colorful robes.

"Can you hear me?" the man on the TV says.

"Are you talking to me?" you ask.

"Yes, I'm taking to you."

"Are you the sorcerer?" you ask.

"No, I am the sorcerer's grandfather."

"Can you tell me how to get out of this maze?"

The old man shakes his head. "No, but I can tell you that in a few moments a whole lot of doors are going to appear and you will have to choose one of them."

"More doors?"

"I'm afraid so."

Then the TV turns off again.

When you turn around, sure enough six doors have appeared.

But which one do you choose?

There are so many.

Do you choose the:
Red door **P76**
Purple door **P82**
Orange door **P79**
Wooden door **P83**
Copper door **P91**
Yellow door **P114**

You have chosen to open the copper door

"Hello again," the sorcerer's apprentice says. "Did you miss me?"

"A bit?" you say. "It seems to have taken ages to get here. I took a few wrong turns."

"Well you've done better than most, so don't complain."

"So what now?" you ask. "Have I got far to go?"

"No not at all," the boy says. "This is the last stage. If you get this right, you might get to meet the sorcerer."

"I'm not sure I want to meet him after all he's put me through," you say. "So, is this the last question?"

"How did you guess?" the boy says.

You sigh preparing for what surely must be the hardest question of all.

"Ready?"

You nod.

"Good luck!"

"Thanks."

"Right. How many cards are in a pack of playing cards, not counting the jokers?"

"Just regular playing cards?" you ask.

The boy nods and gives you a big grin. "Think hard," the boys says.

"Don't worry I will," you reply.

"Work it out by going through the pack if you have to. If you get this wrong ... well I suspect you know what will happen. You'll be back at the very beginning of the maze and have to start over."

You take your time before you answer.

"Remember there are four suits," the apprentice says.

It is time to answer. Are there:

50 cards in a pack? **P83**

Or

52 cards in a pack? **P95**

You have decided to go through the hole in the wall

The hole is dark and you can't see much. You walk forward slowly, feeling the way as you go. The wall feels cold and rough like rock. You wonder if you've entered a cave.

As you walk, it gets warmer and warmer. Where have you ended up?

There is a rumbling beneath your feet. It's an earthquake.

When you see lava running down the tunnel towards you, you realize you're in a lava tube and the volcano is erupting! You've got to get out of here fast!

You turn and run wondering where to go.

Then you see a junction you didn't see on the way in. You must have passed it in the gloom.

Lava hisses behind you. You can feel its heat on your back.

Which way do you go? Do you:

Go left? **P115**

Or

Go right? **P94**

You have decided to go right

As you head further down the tunnel the floor gets steeper and steeper. Before you know it, you are running so fast you're not sure you could stop even if you wanted to.

Thankfully, after another fifty yards the tunnel levels out and comes to an end. You can hear the sizzling lava behind you. But where can you go? What can you do?

A voice booms through the tunnel. "Look up!"

Then you see it. A rope is hanging from the ceiling. It has big knots tied in it to help you climb up. You grab hold and start climbing just as the lava flows under you.

It is hot. Your hands sweat as you climb. You feel like you're about to be roasted alive when you come to a small ledge with two doors set back into it.

One of the doors is made of silver and shines brightly in the light. The other looks like solid gold.

But which do you choose? Do you:

Go through the door made silver? **P117**

Or

Go through the door made of gold? **P95**

Congratulations, you made it to the end of the maze

The last room is like nothing you've ever seen. Shelves of books tower to the sky. High above, a flock of birds circle amongst the clouds.

In the middle of the room the boy sits at a large desk. He is dressed in colorful robes and has a pointy cap on. A jumble of books are open on the desk in front of him.

"I'm pleased to see you finally made it," he says.

You nod and then look around. "So where's the sorcerer?"

The boy snaps his fingers. "Abracadabra!" In a puff of pink smoke, a box of chocolates plops onto the desk in front of you. "Like some chocolate?"

You look at his beaming grin. "You mean you were the sorcerer all along?"

He waves his wand and a big leather chair appears. "Please take a seat and I'll explain."

The chair is huge and soft, like sitting on a cloud.

"Sorry for deceiving you, but I need more apprentices. You see I have so many mazes to make I'm having to do 100 jobs at once."

You could get angry, but what's the point. Besides, the chocolates are the best you've ever tasted. "So why didn't you tell me the truth from the beginning?" you ask.

The boy smiles. "I wanted you to see how much fun it is being an apprentice. You'd have gotten all nervous if you knew I was the sorcerer."

You think back to all the adventures you've had. "It was kind of fun. But why did you care?"

The sorcerer gives you a serious look as he leans forward. "I was hoping you might like to become an apprentice." He snaps his fingers and a fluffy kitten lands on your lap. "There are lots of perks you know and to tell you the truth, I could really do with some help."

You must admit you're interested. Going through the maze was a lot of fun and becoming one of the sorcerer's apprentices would be exciting. "What would I have to do?"

"You'd help make up the questions for my maze. And every now and then you get to act as guide for someone new. Like I did for you as you went through."

"I can think of lots of cool questions," you say. "Did you know that lava can get up to 1100 degrees Celsius?"

"Hmm… interesting," he says. "You sound like a natural."

The sorcerer stands up. "Look, you don't have to make your mind up right now. Have a think about it and if you want to apply for the job let me know. You can apply at my website. You know, I think we could become good friends."

You grab another chocolate and give the kitten a pat.

"I'd better get back to work," the sorcerer says. "I've a million interesting facts to look up."

And with that, the sorcerer disappears. In a puff of marshmallow smelling smoke you find yourself back at home, smarter than you were when you left. You find yourself thinking of all the interesting questions and riddles you'll make up if you decide to become the sorcerer's apprentice.

THE END

Please remember to review this book on Amazon.

Reviews help other readers decide if the book is right for them.

Thanks,

The Sorcerer

Would you like to read some free previews of some other You Say Which Way Adventure Quizzes?

Yes **P105**

Or

Check out the list of choices to make sure you've not missed parts of the story. **P100**

List of Choices

ENTER THE MAZE	1
YOU HAVE CHOSEN JUPITER	4
YOU HAVE CHOSEN SATURN	5
WELCOME BACK TO LEVEL 1	6
YOU HAVE CHOSEN BLUE WHALE	7
YOU HAVE CHOSEN ELEPHANT	8
AN AFRICAN ELEPHANT WEIGHS 4000 TO 7000 KG	9
STARFISH ARE A TYPE OF FISH	10
YOU HAVE CHOSEN NO, STARFISH AREN'T FISH	11
YOU HAVE DECIDED THAT IT'S 14 MILES TO SHORE	13
YOU HAVE CHOSEN 56, 44 AND 100	14
YOU HAVE CHOSEN 64, 44 AND 90	15
YOU HAVE DECIDED THAT IT'S 15 MILES TO SHORE	16
THERE ARE 260 DEGREES ON A COMPASS	18
YOU HAVE CHOSEN 180	20

WELCOME TO LEVEL TWO   22

MT. EVEREST WAS FIRST CLIMBED IN 1993   24

WELCOME BACK TO LEVEL TWO   25

MT. EVEREST WAS FIRST CLIMBED IN 1953   26

YOU HAVE CHOSEN STAMP   28

OOPS. THE RIGHT ANSWER IS STAMP   30

YOU HAVE CHOSEN VULCAN AND MARTIAN   31

YOU HAVE CHOSEN ITALIAN AND AUSTRALIAN   33

YOU HAVE CHOSEN AFRICA   35

YOU HAVE CHOSEN NORTH AMERICA   37

PIZZA WAS INVENTED IN THE UNITED STATES   39

SURPRISE!   41

YIPPEE, YOU GET TO HAVE SOME PIZZA!   43

YOU HAVE CHOSEN TIGER   45

YOU HAVE CHOSEN LEOPARD   46

YOU HAVE CHOSEN THAT THE BOX HAS 6 WALLS 48

OH NO, YOU'VE GONE ALL THE WAY BACK TO LEVEL 1 49

YOU HAVE CHOSEN THAT THAT BOX HAS 4 WALLS 50

WELCOME TO LEVEL 3 51

YOU HAVE CHOSEN BRAZIL 53

YOU HAVE CHOSEN THE AMAZON 55

YOU HAVE CHOSEN SPIDER MONKEY 57

OOPS, THAT IS NOT THE NAME OF A MONKEY 59

YOU HAVE CHOSEN THE WRONG RIVER 60

YOU HAVE CHOSEN VENEZUELA 63

YOU CHOSE $8 PER HOUR 65

YOU HAVE CHOSEN THE WRONG NUMBER 67

YOU HAVE CORRECTLY CHOSEN NUMBER 9 68

YOU ARE BACK AT THE START 70

COAL IS MADE FROM ANCIENT TREES AND PLANTS 71

ALASKA WAS TAKEN FROM JAPAN AT THE END OF WWII   73

WELCOME TO LEVEL 4   74

YOU HAVE CHOSEN THE RED DOOR   76

YOU HAVE CHOSEN THE GREEN DOOR   77

YOU HAVE CHOSEN THE YELLOW DOOR   78

YOU HAVE CHOSEN THE ORANGE DOOR   79

YOU HAVE PUSHED THE UP BUTTON   80

YOU HAVE PUSHED THE DOWN BUTTON   81

YOU HAVE CHOSEN THE PURPLE DOOR   82

YOU ARE BACK IN THE HALLWAY OF DOORS   83

YOU HAVE CHOSEN TO CLIMB THE LADDER   84

YOU HAVE CHOSEN THE BLACK DOOR   85

YOU HAVE CHOSEN THE BROWN DOOR   86

YOU HAVE CHOSEN THE WHITE DOOR   87

YOU HAVE DECIDED TO GO THROUGH THE TRAP DOOR   88

GO THROUGH THE DOOR WITH THE BLUE STRIPES 89

YOU HAVE CHOSEN TO OPEN THE COPPER DOOR 91

GO THROUGH THE HOLE IN THE WALL 93

YOU HAVE DECIDED TO GO RIGHT 94

END OF THE MAZE 95

PLEASE REMEMBER TO REVIEW THIS BOOK ON AMAZON. 99

LIST OF CHOICES 100

FREE BONUS PREVIEWS 105

PREVIEW: THE SORCERER'S MAZE - JUNGLE TREK 105

PREVIEW: THE SORCERER'S MAZE - TIME MACHINE 107

MORE 'YOU SAY WHICH WAY' ADVENTURES 113

Free Bonus Previews

Preview: The Sorcerer's Maze - Jungle Trek

One moment you were at home reading a book and now you're standing in the jungle, deep in the Amazon rainforest.

Beside you flows a slow-moving river, murky brown from all the silt it carries downstream. Monkeys screech in the tall trees across the water. The air is hot and buzzing with insects. As you watch, the tiny flying creatures gather together in an unnatural cloud formation and then separate to form words:

WELCOME they spell in giant letters.

This is crazy you think.

NOPE, IT'S NOT CRAZY spell the insects. THIS IS THE START OF THE SORCERER'S MAZE.

The insect cloud bursts apart and the tiny creatures buzz off. What's next, you wonder?

Twenty yards away two kids, about your age, stand beside a small boat with a small outboard motor attached to its stern. The boat has a blue roof to protect its occupants from the hot tropical sun.

They both smile and wave.

The girl walks towards you. "Do you want a ride up river?" she asks. "My brother and I know the Amazon well."

"Do you work for the sorcerer?" you ask. "He designed the maze, didn't he?"

The girl nods. "Yes. My brother and I are his apprentices.

The sorcerer wants you to have company while you're here."

The two of you walk back down to the river's edge.

"This is Rodrigo. I'm Maria."

You drop your daypack into the dugout and hold out your hand. "Hi Rodrigo, interesting looking boat."

Rodrigo shakes your hand. "It does the job. But before we can go upriver," he says, pulling a piece of paper out of his pocket. "The sorcerer wants me to ask you a question. If you get it right, we can leave."

"And if not?" you ask.

"I've got more questions," the boy says, patting his pocket. "I'm sure you'll get one right eventually." He unfolds the paper. "Okay, here's your first question. Which of the following statements is true?"

It is time to make a decision. Which do you choose?

The Amazon River has over 3000 known species of fish.

Or

The Amazon River has less that 1000 known species of fish.

Preview: The Sorcerer's Maze - Time Machine

The door is ajar so Matilda gives it a shove and walks into the laboratory. "Hey," she says over her shoulder, "come and look at this."

"Are we allowed?" you ask, stepping cautiously through the doorway. "This area's probably off limits."

"I didn't see a sign," Matilda says, rubbing a finger along the edge of a stainless steel bench as she proceeds further into the brightly lit room. "And if they're going to leave the door open…"

Matilda is a foreign exchange student at your school. She's adventurous and sometimes a little crazy, but she's interesting and the two of you have become good friends.

The rest of your classmates are back in the cafeteria questioning the tour guide about the research facility while they wait for lunch to be served. When Matilda suggested a quick walk, you never guessed she planned to snoop around.

The lab's benches are crammed with electrical equipment. Wires and cables run like spaghetti between servers and fancy hardware. Lights and gauges flicker and glow.

You move a little further into the room. "What do you think all this stuff does?"

Matilda wanders down the narrow space between two benches, looking intently at the equipment as she goes. "I dunno. But they don't skimp on gear, do they?"

A low hum buzzes throughout the room. Most of the components are large and expensive looking. But near the end of one bench, Matilda spots a few smaller pieces of tech.

She prods a brick-sized black box with a row of green numbers glowing across it. "I wonder what this does." She picks it up.

Tiny lights glow above a circular dial. On the top of the box is an exposed circuit board made of copper and green plastic.

"Looks like an old digital clock," you say pointing at the first number in the row. "See here's the hours and minutes, then the day, the month and the year." You pull out your cell phone and check the time. "Yep. It's spot on."

"That makes sense," Matilda says. "But what's the dial for?"

"Beats me. To set an alarm, maybe?

Matilda rubs her finger along a curved piece of copper tubing fitted neatly into one end of the box. "So what's this coil for? Doesn't look like any timer I've ever seen."

When she turns the box over, there is a sticky label on its bottom. It reads:

Hands Off - Property of the Sorcerer

"Who's the sorcerer?" Matilda asks.

You shrug. "One of the scientists maybe?"

"A sorcerer's a magician, not a scientist." She turns the box back over and starts fiddling with the dial.

You take a step back. "I don't think that's a good—"

A sudden burst of static crackles through the air. The

copper coil glows bright red and there's a high-pitched squeal.

FLASH—BANG!

Pink mist fills the air.

"Crikey!" Matilda says. "What the heck caused that?"

Matilda looms ghostlike through the haze.

"We're in for it now," you say, hoping the smoke alarm doesn't go off. "Someone must have heard that."

But as the mist clears, someone hearing you is the last of your worries. "Where—where's the lab gone?"

You're standing on an open plain, brown and burnt by the blistering sun. In the distance three huge stone structures rise above the shimmering heat haze. Workers swarm over the site like ants on piles of sugar.

Matilda stares, her mouth open, trying to make sense of it all. The black box dangles from her hand. She turns to face you. "Streuth mate! The lab. She—she's completely disappeared!"

"But how? Unless..." You reach down and lift the box so you can check the numbers flashing on its side. "This says it's 11:45."

Matilda nods. "Yeah, that's about right. Just before lunch."

"In the year 2560!"

Matilda's eyes widen. "2560? How can that be?".

"That's 2560 BC," a voice behind you says. "See the little minus sign in front of the numbers?"

The two of you spin around.

"Jeez, mate," Matilda says, glaring at the newcomer. "Where the blazes did you spring from? You nearly scared last night's dinner outta me."

The owner of the voice is a boy about your age, dressed

in white cotton. Bands of gold encircle his wrists. His hair is jet black and cut straight across in the front, like his hairdresser put a bowl on his head.

"I'm the sorcerer's apprentice," he says with a smile. "You've been playing with the sorcerer's time machine haven't you?"

"Time machine?" you and Matilda say in unison.

"Welcome to ancient Egypt. The pyramids are coming along nicely don't you think?"

You glance over towards the structures in the distance then back to the boy. "But how did we—"

"— end up here?" the apprentice says. "When you fiddled with the sorcerer's machine, you bent space-time. In fact you bent it so much, you've ended up in the sorcerer's maze. Now you've got to answer questions and riddles to get out."

Matilda's upper lip curls and her eyes squint, contorting her face into a look of total confusion. "What sorta questions?"

The apprentice reaches out his hand. "Don't worry. The questions aren't difficult. But first you'd better give me that box, before you get yourself in trouble."

"Is answering questions the only way to get back?" you ask.

The boy in white nods then gives you a smile. "Here's how the time maze works. If you answer a question correctly you get to move closer to your own time. But if you get it wrong. I spin the dial and we take our chances."

You gulp. "You mean we could end up anywhere?"

"You mean any-when, don't ya?" Matilda says.

The sorcerer's apprentice chuckles. "I suppose you're right. Anywhere, anytime. It's all the same in the sorcerer's maze."

"But we've got to answer questions to get home?" you repeat. "There's no other way?"

"Sorry, I don't make the rules. I just do what the sorcerer says. At least he's sent me along to help out. That's some consolation, eh?"

"Well... I suppose..."

"Get on with it then," Matilda says in her typical no-nonsense way. "I'm hungry and it's nearly lunchtime."

The boy tucks the black box under his arm, then reaches into a fold of his robe and pulls out a scroll of papyrus. He straightens the scroll and reads. "Okay here goes. The pyramids are about 481 feet high but they weren't used as look out posts or land marks. What was their purpose?"

The apprentice looks at you expectantly. "It's time for your first decision:

Which do you choose?"

Egyptians used pyramids as accommodation for slaves.

Or

The pyramids were used as tombs.

More 'You Say Which Way' Adventures

Danger on Dolphin Island
Pirate Island
In the Magician's House
Creepy House
Dragons Realm
Stranded Starship
Dungeon of Doom
Volcano of Fire
Secrets of Glass Mountain
Mystic Portal
Dinosaur Canyon
Deadline Delivery
Between The Stars
Lost in Lion Country
Once Upon an Island
Danger on Dolphin Island
The Sorcerer's Maze Jungle Trek
The Sorcerer's Maze Time Machine

Oops. The sorcerer is tricky so watch out! Go back to level two **P22**

Oops. The sorcerer is tricky so watch out! Go back to the beginning of the maze. **P1**

Oops, that is incorrect. The sorcerer is tricky so watch out! Go back to level two **P22**

Oops. How did that happen? Go back to the beginning of level three **P51**

YouSayWhichWay.com

Made in the USA
Middletown, DE
19 June 2020